YIKES!

DESK STORIES

BY KEVIN O'MALLEY

ALBERT WHITMAN & COMPANY, CHICAGO, ILLINOIS

Library of Congress Cataloging-in-Publication Data

O'Malley, Kevin, 1961-
Desk stories / by Kevin O'Malley.
v. cm.
Summary: Six separate stories tell, in words and cartoons, the surprising
history and activities of the ordinary school desk.
Contents: History Man—Trapped!—It came from within—Desk time jokes—
Desktec—Sue Smallton.
ISBN 978-0-8075-1562-4
1. Desks—Juvenile fiction. 2. Children's stories, American. 3. Graphic
novels. [1. Graphic novels. 2. Desks—Fiction. 3. Short stories. 4. Humorous stories.] I. Title.
PZ7.7.O43Des 2011
[E]—dc22
2010050423

Published in 2011 by Albert Whitman & Company.

Printed in China,
10 9 8 7 6 5 4 3 2 1 BP 15 14 13 12 11

The design is by Carol Gildar.

For more information about Albert Whitman & Company,
please visit our web site at www.albertwhitman.com.

CONTENTS

I lost
my backpack.

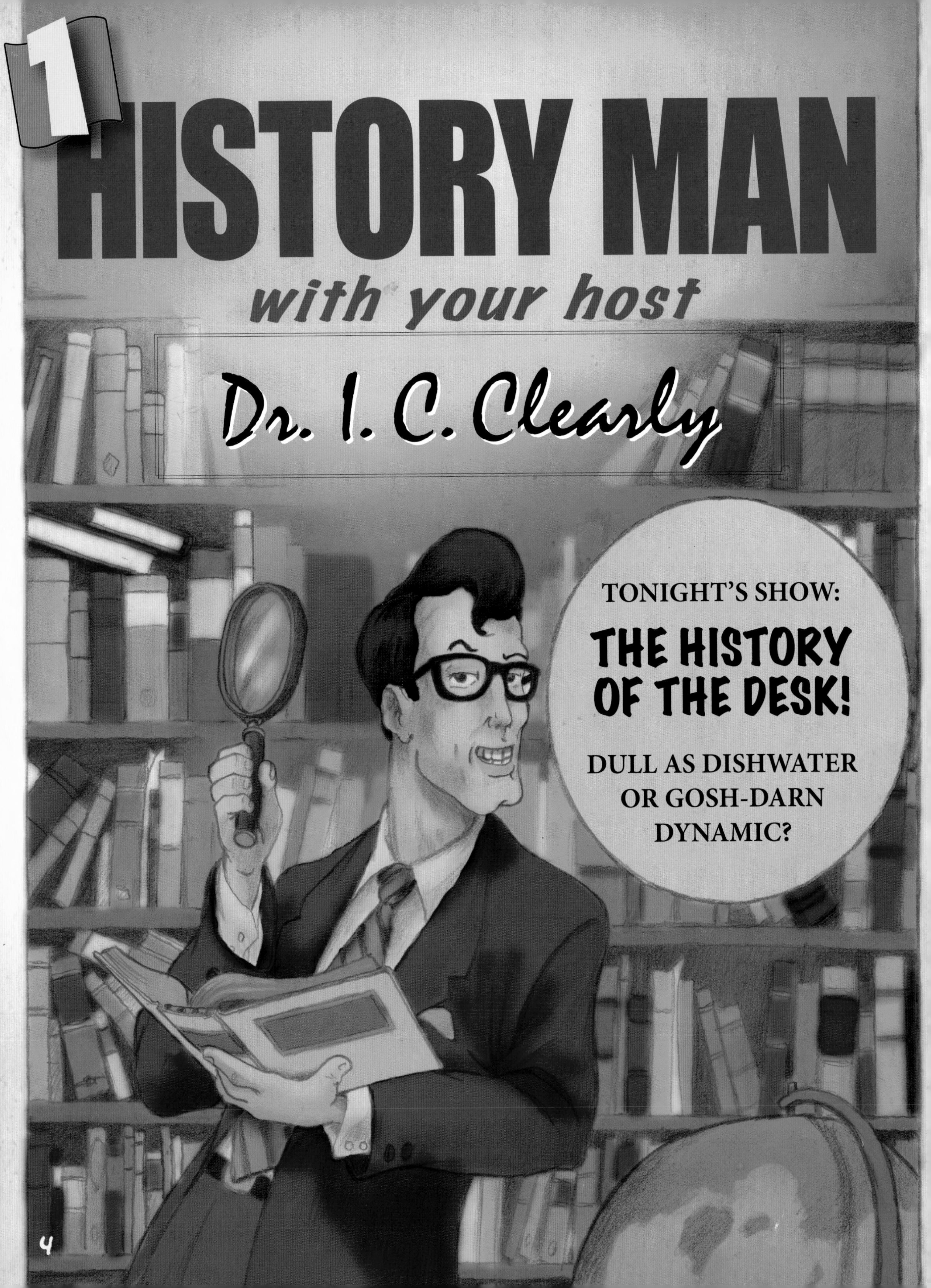

1

HISTORY MAN

with your host

Dr. I. C. Clearly

TONIGHT'S SHOW:

THE HISTORY OF THE DESK!

DULL AS DISHWATER OR GOSH-DARN DYNAMIC?

Every day cave boy Roscoe Jr. went to school. And every day when he went to sit at his boulder, he would stub his toe.
UGH BE WAH NE. (Good morning, Ms. Spear.)
That's when Roscoe Jr. created the first desk.
BA NA WAAA NEG BA YA! (Ouch!)
Roscoe Jr. found a giant flat rock. He sat on his rock chair,
GIB NA VO BA NABBI HO! (I'm so clever!)
and then he put the flat boulder on his lap.
This is also the first time a teacher said, "Stop playing under your desk."
NEV ME ROO ME KE ME KE? (How about a little help here?)
In the Middle Ages students sat at desks that had spikes on the top. They weren't very good desks for writing, but nobody ever, ever, ever fell asleep in class.

In the 1850s students used chalk and erasers on blackboards that they held on their laps.

The system proved troublesome.

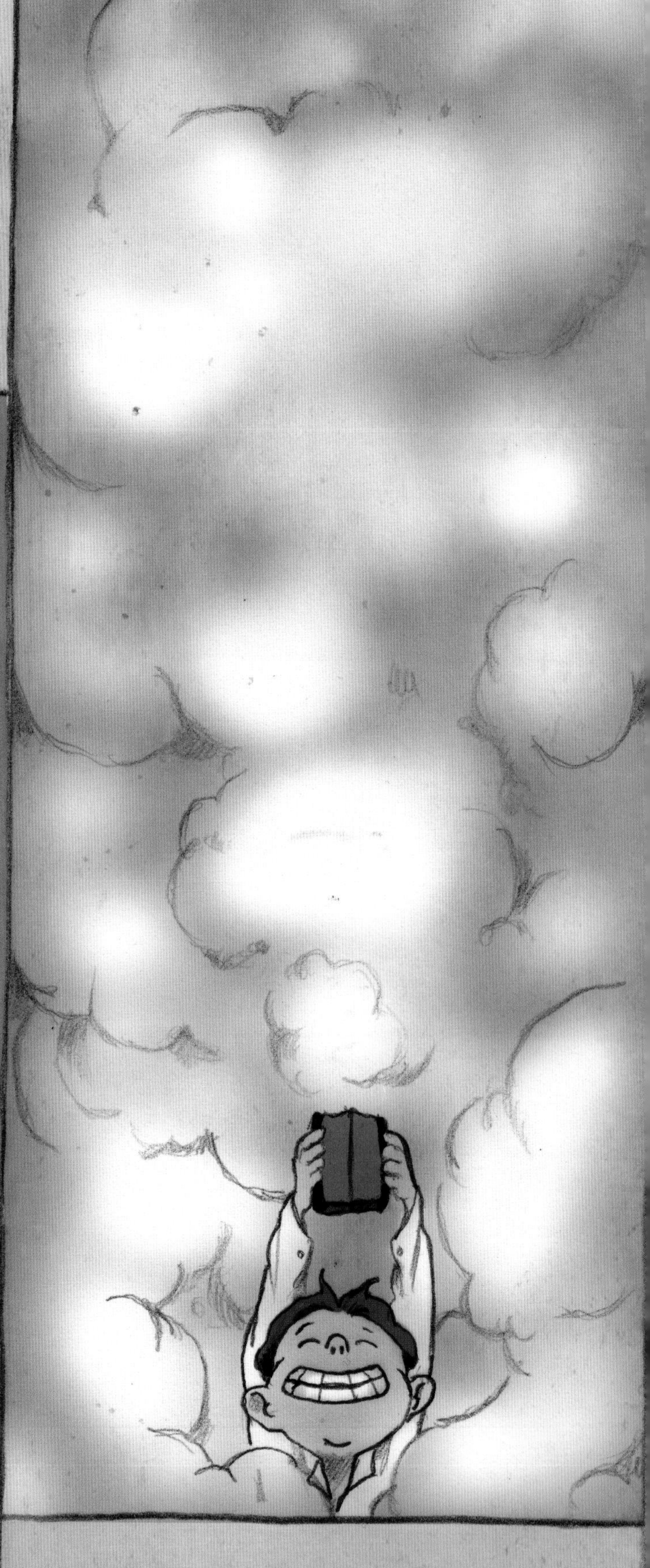

Who would have thought that giving kids erasers could cause such a problem?

Through the years inventors have tried different kinds of desks.

Shockingly Educational
Electro-Stimulator
The desk of the FUTURE!

GROOOVY MAN
The Beanbag
Lose the desk

Outdoor classrooms . . .
Mother Earth is the greatest desk . . . as long as you have **BUGAWAY!**

BUGAWAY

The modern desk, so hard, so unforgiving, so extraordinarily uncomfortable. The only thing that could make it better is SUMMER VACATION!

The End

2 Trapped!

The Sohandsome family was strong and brave, kind and generous.
John was trapped.
On the dangerous voyage to America, they clung to each other for support and blah blah blah blah . . .
Unable to free himself,
Life in the New World was difficult, but they worked hard together and made their farm prosper and blah blah blah blah blah blah blah blah blah blah blah . . .
John fell asleep.
You are my prisoner!
You are wrong, evil desk. I will escape.

Zzzzzzzzz . . .
zzzzzzzz . . .
P.S. 801
I'm FREE!

CRASH!
YIKES!
You will never escape.

The evil desk chased John. It grew bigger and bigger and bigger.
You can run, but you cannot hide!

Now I will swallow you whole.

This is your destiny! HA HA HA!

Just as the evil desk was about to take a bite . . .

John woke up!
NO!

John, please. I know the story is very exciting, but you must not yell in class. Now I'll finish the chapter.

The Sohandsome family sang songs as the storm raged outside, even as the cabin shook so hard they thought it would fall at any moment and blah blah blah blah blah blah blah . . .
The End
John was trapped. There would be no escape.

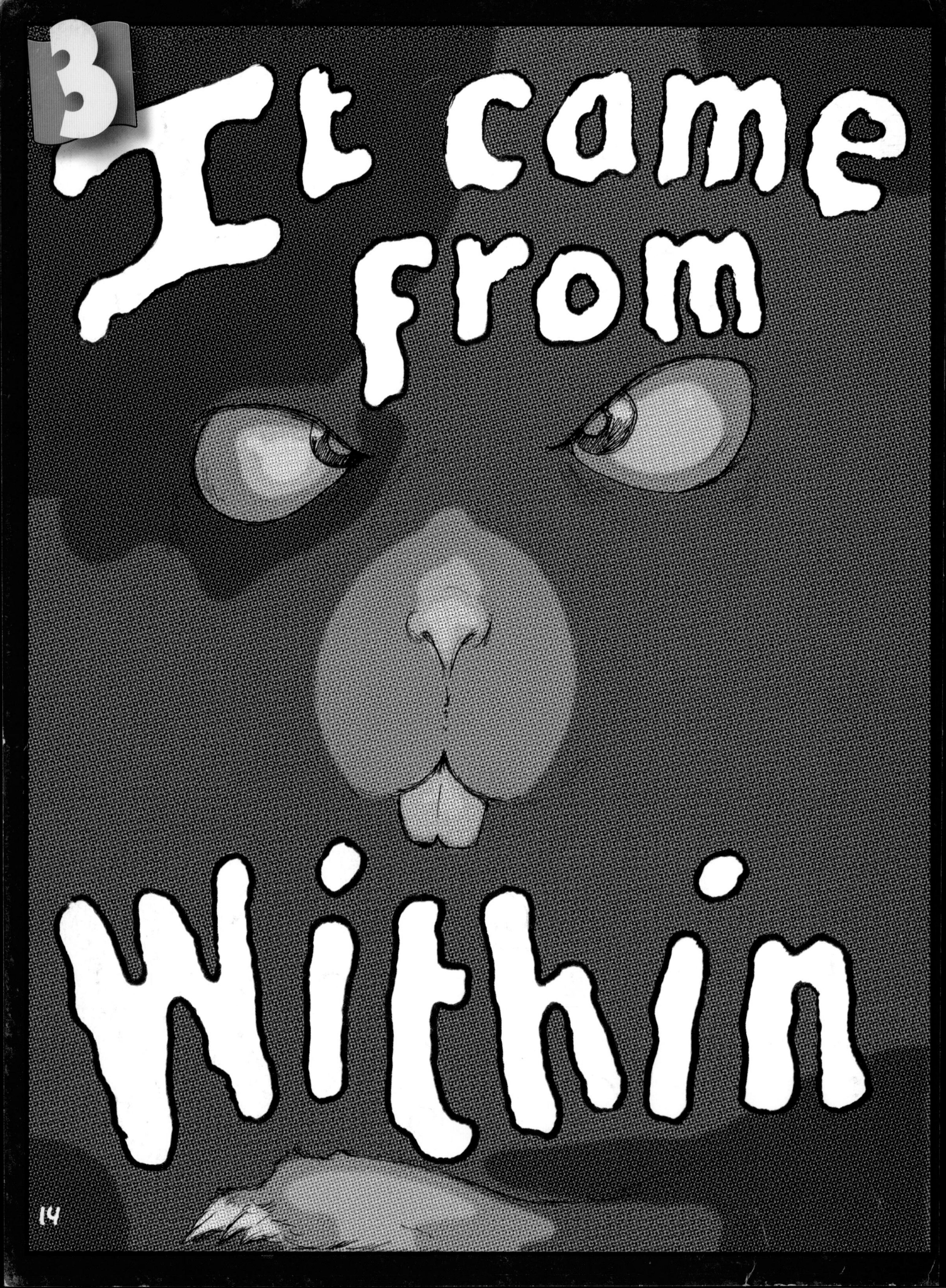
3
It came from Within

Perfect Sara was always prepared. Perfect Sara had perfect hair and perfect clothes. Perfect Sara loved taking tests. She always got a perfect score.

But perfect Sara loved to brag.

"Okay, class," said the teacher. "Take out your pencils and begin the test. You have half an hour."

The class started their tests. But Sara couldn't find her pencil.
She reached way in the back of her desk.
That's when she felt it! It was warm! It was FURRY!
AHHH!
Sara's teacher wasn't happy.
Stop the test . . . MY, MY, MY DESK!
"Here's a pencil, Sara. Now start your test," said the teacher.
But, but, but . . . in my desk . . . something . . .

Sara tried to start the test.
She tried to concentrate,
but the thing in her desk was moving.
The clock was ticking: twenty minutes left.
STOP THE TEST!
Is there a problem?
Maybe you should have studied.
Now Sara's teacher was mad.
But, but, but . . .
"Get back to work, Sara."
But, but, but . . .
"Sara, please, back to work."
But, but, but . . .
The thing was moving again.

Sara bragged that she was always prepared. She bragged that she was always perfect.
But Sara wasn't prepared for the thing in her desk.
The clock was ticking. Ten minutes left in the test.
The thing was scratching. The thing was moving.
Five minutes left in the test. Tick, tick, tick went the clock. The thing was coming out of the desk!
IT'S COMING OUT!

TICK...
TICK...
TICK...
Is there a problem, Sara? You look perfectly crazy.
Oh, this is perfect.

"It looks like our hamster has escaped again," said Sara's teacher.
Perfect Sara knows where the hamster is, Mr. Nutt.
You weren't prepared for that, huh, Sara?
THE END

4
DESK TIME
JOKES
I don't feel well.
Where don't you feel well?
In school.
How do you manage to get so many things wrong?
Well, I always get to school early.
What would you get if you crossed a vampire and a teacher?
Lots of blood tests!
Where is your homework?
A kid fell in a lake. I jumped in to rescue him. Sadly, my homework drowned.

The best part of school is seeing all your friends.
The worst part is your teacher won't let you talk to them.
Name the four seasons.
Salt, pepper, ketchup, and creamy ranch.
From the second I picked up the book until the moment I put it down, I couldn't stop laughing. Someday I plan on reading it.
Why were the early days of history called the Dark Ages?
Because there were so many knights!
Didn't I tell you to stand at the end of the line?
I couldn't. There was already someone there.

5
DESKTEC
WITH
DIRK
SAVAGE,
SUPERGENIUS
TOP
SECRET

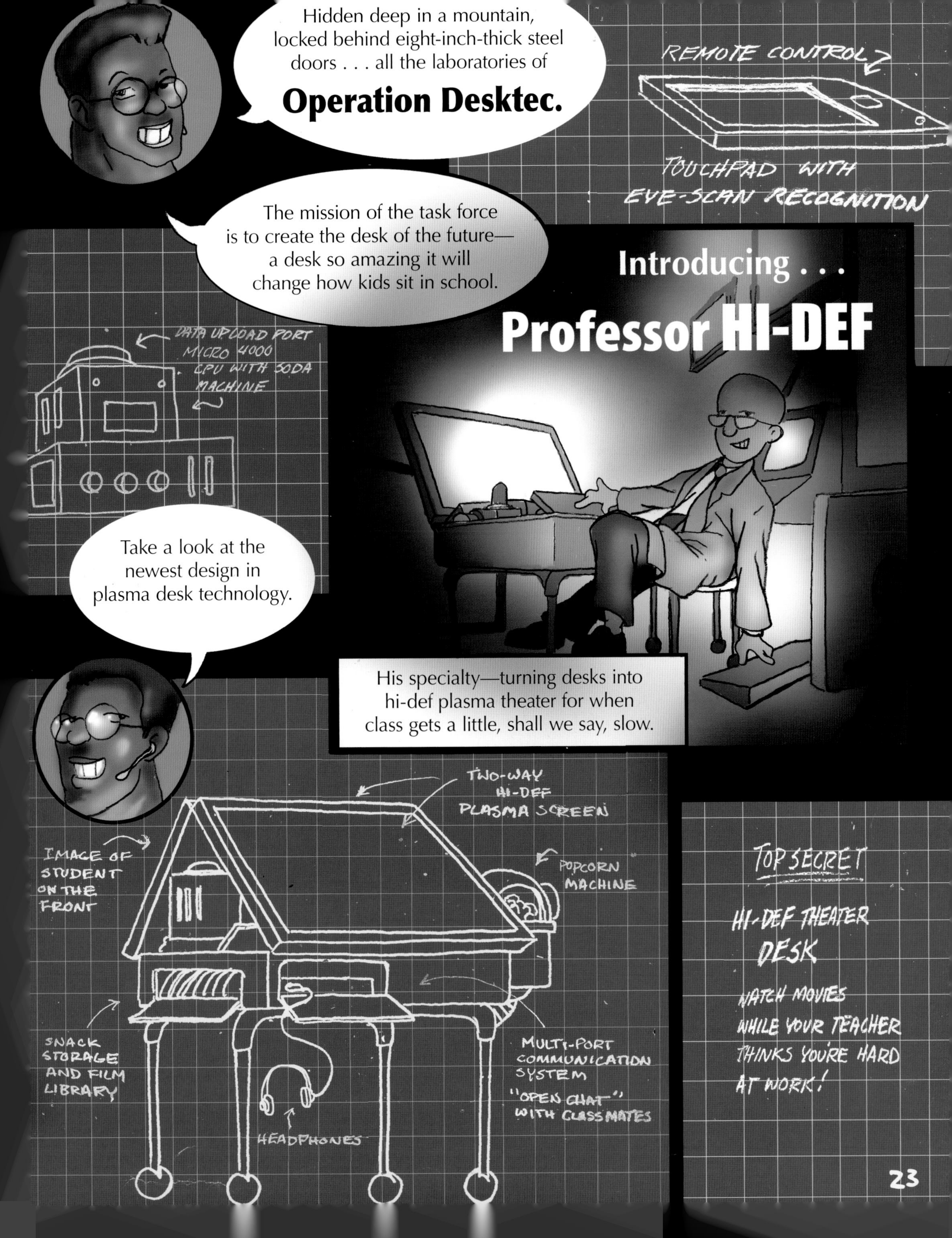

Hidden deep in a mountain, locked behind eight-inch-thick steel doors . . . all the laboratories of
Operation Desktec.
REMOTE CONTROL
TOUCHPAD WITH EYE-SCAN RECOGNITION
The mission of the task force is to create the desk of the future—a desk so amazing it will change how kids sit in school.
Introducing . . .
Professor HI-DEF
DATA UPLOAD PORT
MICRO 4000 CPU WITH SODA MACHINE
Take a look at the newest design in plasma desk technology.
His specialty—turning desks into hi-def plasma theater for when class gets a little, shall we say, slow.
TWO-WAY HI-DEF PLASMA SCREEN
IMAGE OF STUDENT ON THE FRONT
POPCORN MACHINE
TOP SECRET
HI-DEF THEATER DESK
WATCH MOVIES WHILE YOUR TEACHER THINKS YOU'RE HARD AT WORK!
SNACK STORAGE AND FILM LIBRARY
MULTI-PORT COMMUNICATION SYSTEM
"OPEN CHAT" WITH CLASSMATES
HEADPHONES

In the future, your desk won't just sit there waiting for you. No, in the future your desk will go home with you! Backpacks will be history. I'd like you to meet . . .

A good desk is nothing without a chair, so Desktec hires only the best designers. Leading our chair design division is the amazing . . .

THE ALL-TERRAIN FOUR-WHEEL DRIVE DESK

Snow, rain, hurricane . . . You'll never forget your homework again.

CAPTAIN COMFORT

Take a look at the new 3000zb.

And what do I do? I have the hardest job of all . . .

My job is to get your teacher to buy one!
Good morning, Ms. Wright. You look lovely today.
THE END

6
Sue Smallton
The Incredible Shrinking Supergirl

Sue Smallton was just a regular girl sitting at her desk.
Suddenly, Claire McBrat walked up. "Sue, I need that barrette I lent you last week."
No problem, Claire . . . It's in my desk.
Sue Smallton pushed the secret button on her belt
and became . . .
The Incredible Shrinking Supergirl!
I'm going in!

Without any fear, the Incredible Shrinking Supergirl walked into the gaping mouth of her desk,

over broken pencils,

and past disgusting, crumbly, chewed-up, slightly wet erasers.

It grew darker and darker and darker.

Suddenly the Incredible Shrinking Supergirl was attacked by her dictionary.

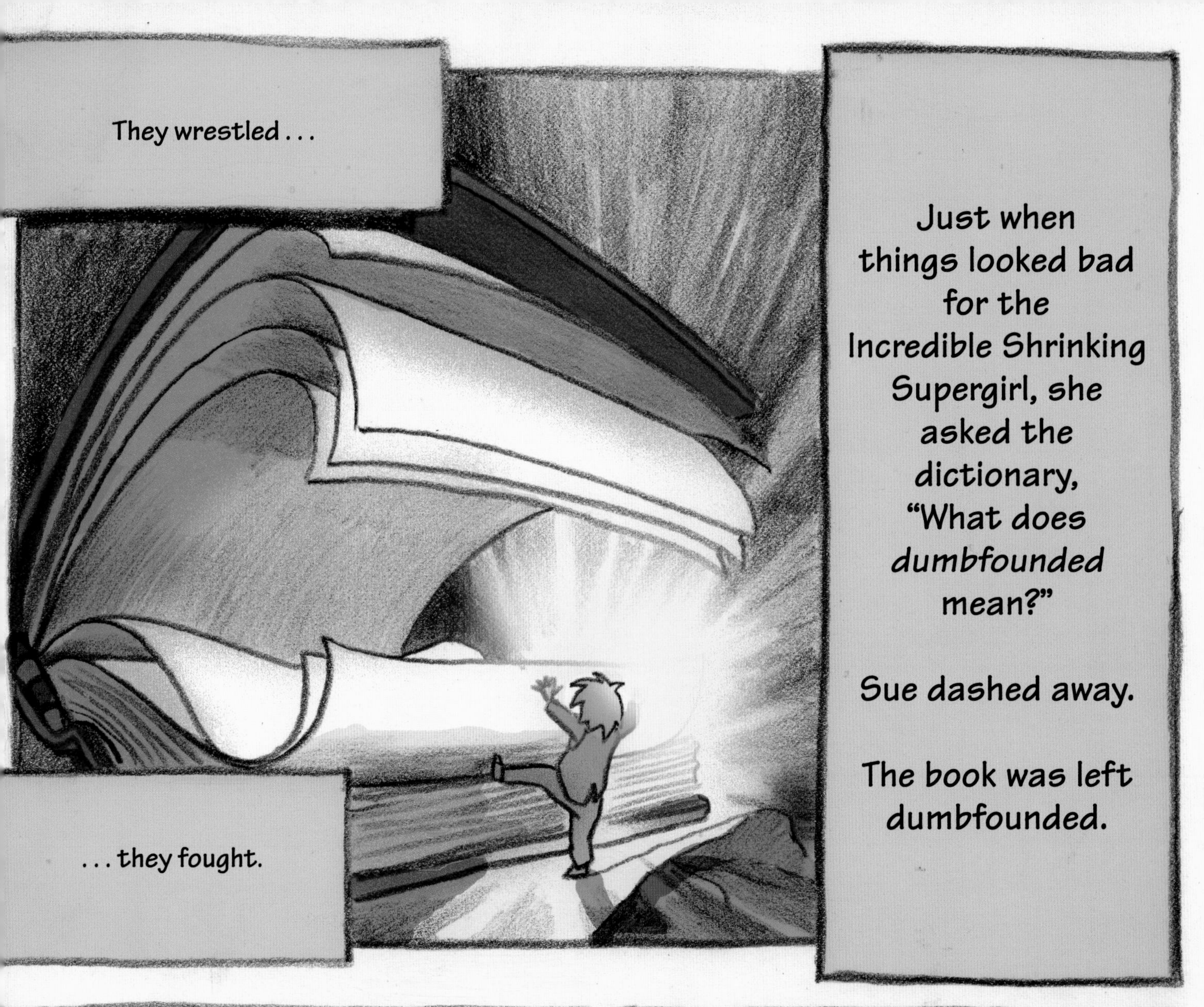
They wrestled . . .
. . . they fought.
Just when things looked bad for the Incredible Shrinking Supergirl, she asked the dictionary, "What does *dumbfounded* mean?"
Sue dashed away.
The book was left dumbfounded.

The Incredible Shrinking Supergirl crept over notes for her mom and dad, flyers for upcoming school events, and less-than-good test papers,
over her mountain of a math book,
and her hideously huge history of America!

The Incredible Shrinking Supergirl could see the barrette! She took a step forward and picked it up. (It was a little sticky and covered in hair.)

Suddenly she was attacked by an old piece of gum . . . the worst kind . . . BLUEBERRY!

The Incredible Shrinking Supergirl raced back to the opening of the desk. The gum was close behind.

With all her mighty strength, the Incredible Shrinking Supergirl leaped from the desk . . .

. . . YYYYEEE-AAAHHH!

THE BARRETTE WAS SAVED!!!

Oh yeah, baby, I'm good!
That's disgusting. It's all sticky and hairy, Sue!
The End!

WHERE DO YOU THINK YOU'RE GOING?
ON SUMMER VACATION . . . CAN YOU GIVE ME A PUSH OUT THE DOOR?

CRASH!
You are doomed!